AUTHOR

Jessie Wee has had 12 years of teaching experience, both in Primary and Secondary schools. Since giving up teaching, she has been writing children's stories, over a 100 of which have appeared in children's magazines. THE ADVENTURES OF MONTY is her first collection of stories to be published in book form.

ILLUSTRATOR

Kwan Shan Mei, a gifted artist, has set a very high standard for herself in the illustrations she does for children's books. This Shanghai-educated artist has done a short period of understudy with the great master Chow Han Mei. She has developed a varied style and always strives to bring out the essential character in each of her drawings.

The adventures of Monty
Monty Moves Out

Story by Jessie Wee
Pictures by Kwan Shan Mei

FEDERAL PUBLICATIONS
Singapore • Kuala Lumpur • Hong Kong

© 1987 Federal Publications (S) Pte Ltd
Times Jurong
2 Jurong Port Road
Singapore 2261

First published 1987

ISBN 9971 4 1428 7

Printed in Singapore by Koon Wah Printing Pte Ltd

for my sons
ANDY and DEREK

Monty left Grandma's house early in the morning.

He walked sadly down the empty street carrying only
his bag and his little stool.

He walked on and on until he was tired.
At last he came to a green field.
He walked under the coconut trees
and then he stopped.

In front of him was a huge tree.
It had such bright, red flowers that
it looked as though it was on fire!

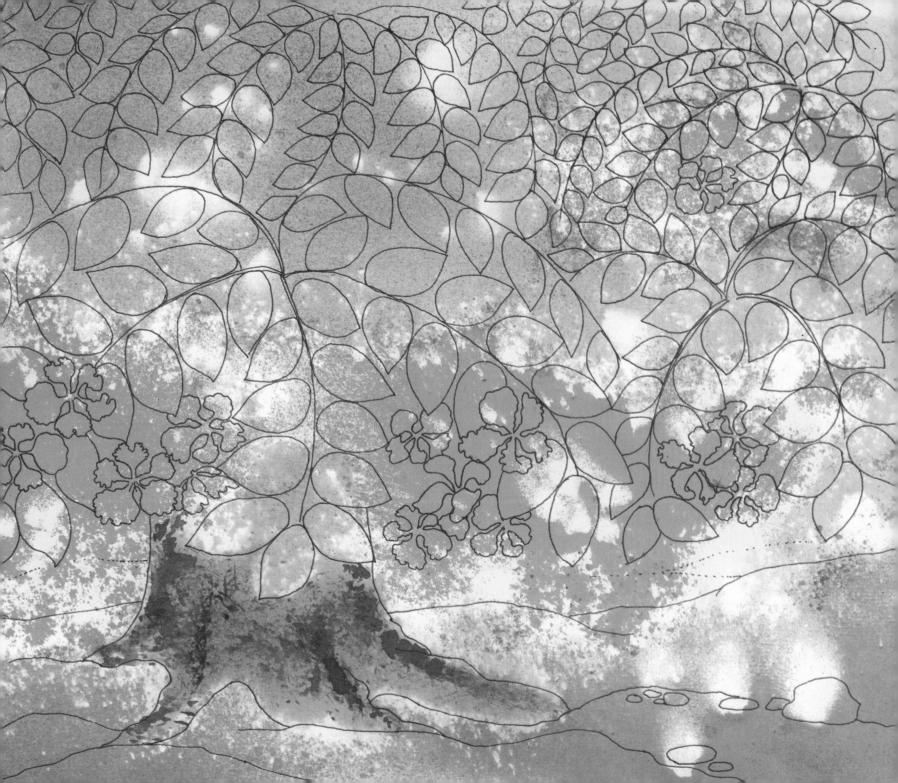

Monty moved closer and there
he saw a dear little house
in the hollow of the tree.

"I shall stay here," Monty said.
"This will be my new home!"

Monty climbed into his new home.

Monty liked his new home.
He liked the huge tree
  with its bright, red flowers.
He liked the green field.

He wanted to sweep out the dry, brown leaves
  from his home.
He wanted his new home to be clean and tidy,
  but poor Monty was so tired, he fell fast asleep
  on top of all the brown leaves.

When Monty awoke, the sun was shining
on his bed of leaves.
Monty jumped up and ran to the door.

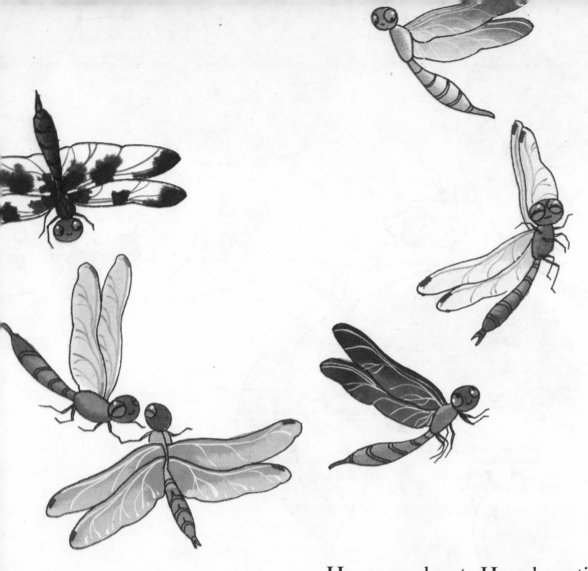

He peeped out. How beautiful everything was!

Monty took a deep breath and stayed to watch
the dragonflies dancing in the air.

He watched the busy ants
walking up and down the branch.
He watched the baby lizards
playing hide-and-seek among the leaves.

Monty laughed as he watched the baby lizards.
The baby lizards heard Monty and they stopped playing.
The busy ants heard Monty and they all stood still.

The dragonflies heard Monty and they flew
round and round in circles.

They all looked very alarmed.

"Please don't run away!"
Monty cried out. "I won't
hurt you!"

Everyone looked at Monty in surprise.
"Why, you're a little mouse!"
they all cried out together.

Monty nodded. "I'm Monty
and I'm all alone.
Please let me be your friend!"

The baby lizards, the ants and the dragonflies
stared at Monty.
They did not know what to say and each waited
for the other to speak.

Suddenly, they heard a loud splash!
It came from the pond on the other side
   of the field.
The dragonflies buzzed excitedly
   as they flew towards the pond.

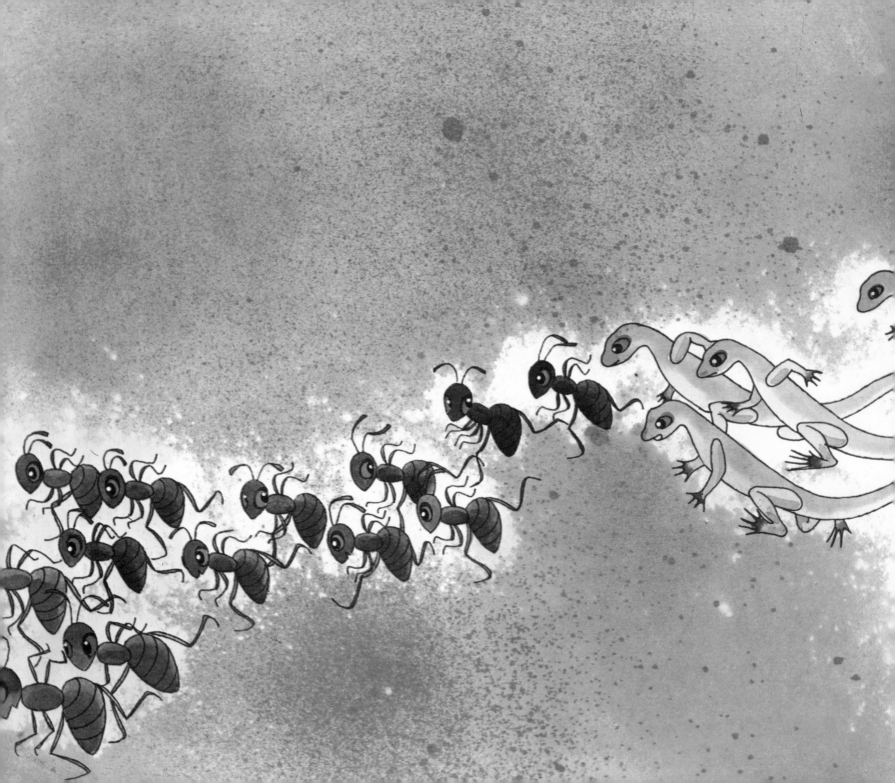

The ants ran down the tree towards the pond.
The baby lizards ran after the ants, and poor Monty
    who did not want to be left alone, ran after them.
They all ran to the pond as fast as their legs
    could carry them.

Soon . . . . everyone was running to the pond.
There, they saw the frogs jumping up and down in fear.

"Help! Help!" cried Mother Bird.
"My baby has fallen into the pond!"

Mother Bird did not know what to do.
The frogs did not know what to do.
All the animals did not know what to do.

Only Monty knew what to do.

"Catch my tail," cried Monty.

"Catch Monty's tail," cried the lizards.

"Catch Monty's tail," cried the frogs.

"Catch Monty's tail," cried Mother Bird.

Baby Bird caught hold of Monty's tail.
Mother Bird caught hold of Monty's paws.
All the animals ran to help.
They pulled and pulled until Baby Bird was
   safely out of the water.

"Thank you, Monty," cried Mother Bird.
"Thank you, Monty," cried Baby Bird.
"Thank you, Monty," cried all the animals
as they came to pat his back.

Monty was a hero!
The ants, the baby lizards and
    the dragonflies were proud of him.
"Monty is our friend," they cried.
Monty was very happy.